CW01044694

Diary of a Horny Wife:
My Sexy Photo Shoot

BY GG

Copyright © 2014 Marriage Heat Publishing

All rights reserved.

ISBN-13:
978-1496045805
ISBN-10:
1496045807

DEDICATION

To my loving husband,

Ben, I dedicate this work of love to you. For thirty years now, you have been my love. The father of our three wonderful children and of course my lovr.

Thank you for being you and for loving me for all these years. Without you ,this would never have happened. You are my fantasy and my reality. I love you with all my being.

Your loving wife; Gina

CONTENTS

ACKNOWLEDGMENTS

A special Thanks to Blondie and Ladygarden for their support and treasured advice. Thank you and God bless you both, my friends. Keep it horny!

The Plan

I am 100% unequivocally in love with my husband. He is more than just my husband. He is my best friend, my confidante, the father of our three wonderful children and my lover. He is mine and I am his. He is my fantasy. He is my reality. I thank the good Lord every day for bringing this man in my life.

December 25th

We had a wonderful Christmas! It was such a blessing to be able to spend it with family and friends. Everyone had a great time exchanging gifts, singing Christmas carols and pigging out on good food, all in the celebration of the birth of our Lord and Savior Jesus Christ.

The down side was: Ben had to leave for New Orleans the day after Christmas and wouldn't be back till New Year's day or so.

Christmas night, once the party was over and

the clean up was completed, Ben and I headed for bed. We made love. It wasn't wild or kinky, it was just soft gentle lovemaking in the missionary position. We gazed into each other's eyes as he thrust his hard cock into my hungry wet pussy. I loved it! He was so hard and it felt so good, the look on our faces showed our passion as we spoke our words of passion to one another.

"*I'm cumming*! Oh, Ben, baby, I'm *cumming*!" I panted into his ear as my body exploded with an orgasm.

Ben smiled as my body trembled and twitched beneath him. He began to thrust a little harder and faster, deep grunts and groans escaped his lips as he pounded my cunt with his big hard dick. I could tell he was getting close to his release and worked my hips feverishly to meet his thrusts (after 30 years you learn things!).

"Gina! Baby, talk to me! Talk to me, my dirty girl! Oh, baby, your pussy is so hot and wet!" Ben groaned.

"Mm-mph! You make me hot and wet, baby! Love me! Fuck my hot little pussy! Baby, your dick feels so good! Love me till you cum deep inside me! *Cum for me, my big-dicked stud*!" I panted as I ran my nails lightly up and down his back.

"*I'm gonna cum!* I'm gonna...gr-r-r-r-rumph! " He growled as his body tensed and trembled. His dick pulsated inside me as it spewed forth his seed deep into me.

I wrapped my legs around him and held him inside me.

"I love you!" I panted softly into his ear. We lay that way for several minutes before he finally slipped out of me.

"I love you! I love you so much!" He said with a smile as I lay in his arms, my head on his chest. I slept in his arms the rest of the night. Merry Christmas indeed!

December 26th

Ben left for New Orleans around 7am. As we kissed, I really didn't want to let go! I wanted to keep him home with me. As much as I hated it, the fact was he needed to go to work, that was the reality.

"I love you. Call me when you get there! Be careful, okay?" I said giving him another quick kiss.

"I will. I love you too, baby!" Ben replied. He gave me a gentle pat on the ass, got into his truck and drove away.

I went back into the house and began packing away some Christmas decor. I generally leave my tree up till New Years day. As I packed I began to smile as I thought of how blessed I am to have a wonderful loving husband and three great kids. The Lord has definitely blessed me.

Ben has worked so hard over the years and has been such an awesome husband and father. He is a big man, but also has a big heart. He cried when his father passed away, as we all did. He cried at the birth of each of our children and when they were baptized.

He is the man who made me a woman all those years ago. He is a wonderful lover and continues to bring passion to our love bed. The orgasms I have when we make love are so much sweeter than any I could give myself. He truly completes me.

I decided I wanted to do something special for him. I wasn't quite sure what. I thought about maybe fixing his favorite meal and then making love to him by candlelight all night long. I thought about a lot of different ideas, all of which sounded good, but I still couldn't decide what I wanted to do.

After fixing my son Randy a bite to eat. I grabbed my laptop and logged into the Marriage Heat website. I began working on a story that I had started. It was then that I remembered something my dear friend, Ladygarden, a fellow poster on the site, had commented on Marriage Heat, about the time she had a photographer friend of hers take some nude photos of her for her husband. She'd put them into an album and sent it to her dear hubby who was away at work.

This idea intrigued me and I will admit aroused me quite a bit. Ben has several pictures of me on his cell, in various states of undress and poses. He masturbates to them while he is away. He calls them his "Emergency Relief Kit". The more I thought about it, the more I liked the idea.

I immediately thought of my friend and former salon client, Shelly. She is a professional photographer and has her own studio in town. She took the photos at my and Ben's 30th anniversary vow renewal ceremony. She did an awesome job.

I decided to give her a call. I was nervous, as I didn't know how she would react to my request. If she declined, then the nude photo idea would be a bust. I knew of no other photographer, at least not one I would trust or feel comfortable with taking such personal pictures of me. I wasn't even sure how to ask her.

My heart was racing as she answered the phone after four or five rings. I decided to just come on out with it, "Could you do a nude photo shoot of me for my husband?"

She paused for a moment then said, "Sure, girl, we can do that! Do you want to do partial or full nudes?"

I took a deep sigh of relief, and then said, "I was thinking some of both!"

"So where and when do you want to do this? I can come to your house and set up there or we can do it at my studio after I close up?"

Home would be where I felt I would be more comfortable, but I have a fifteen-year-old to consider. "I guess we can do it at your studio. Just whenever is good for you. Next week would probably be best," I said.

"Okay, how about a week from Friday, that will be January 3rd? I close around 4:30 or so, you can come then or anytime after. I will wait for ya! How does that sound?" Shelly asked.

"Sounds great! I guess I will see you then!" I replied.

"Maybe we can get together before hand for lunch and discuss a few details? I have a few ideas in mind you might like. Ok, GG guess I will talk to ya later then," Shelly said.

As I hung up the phone I smiled. My excitement of what I had just arranged built inside me. *Wow! Am I really gonna do this? Can I really do this?* I thought to myself. Butterflies built in my stomach and a tingle ran through my warm and moistened cunt.

A thought then ran through my mind. Many of the photos of me that Ben has in his phone, I have my legs spread (per his request). It was one thing to pose that way as he took the pictures, but it was another thing entirely to do such photos while someone else takes the pictures. I couldn't dare ask Shelly to take photos of me that she might find offensive. Or could I? If I was going to do this, I wanted the pictures to be beautiful and erotic, not just "wife porn". However I knew Ben got aroused by such pictures of me, why else would he ask me to pose for him in this manner if he didn't? Now the butterflies really kicked in.

My son Randy walked into the room and I asked him if he wanted to go get something to eat and maybe go to the mall. He agreed. I was glad cause I needed to take my mind off of my pending plans and calm my nerves.

We ate and then walked around the mall for a couple hours. It was really busy as it usually is the day after Christmas. After leaving the mall, we stopped in at my dearest friend Cynthia's house on the way home.

Cynthia and I talked girl-talk and enjoyed some wine, while Randy and her son Billy went out to ride four wheelers. We talked about a variety of subjects, mainly friendly gossip, our husbands and, yes, sex. Hey, what else do two married gals have to talk about?

She was very supportive when I told her of my upcoming photo shoot. She said she would consider doing something like it for her hubby, if she had the nerve. I still wasn't sure I really had the nerve.

We visited for around three hours before I headed home. Randy stayed, deciding he wanted to spend the night. I went home and grabbed him a change of clothes to take back to him, before heading home to stay.

The house was quiet and dark when I finally made it home. I clicked on the television and went to the kitchen and poured myself another glass of wine, then plopped down on the sofa. I had quite the buzz by the time I decided to go and take my shower.

I undressed and started my shower water. Before stepping in, I looked at myself in the full-length mirror that hung on the bathroom door. I was proud of my body and worked hard to keep it fit and looking nice. It seems as I get older the harder I have to work at it.

Child bearing had left a few stretch marks but otherwise I was pleased. Hey, my boobs were still fairly firm, though I've often wished they were a tad bigger. I have large dark areoles and large sensitive nipples. I have nice-looking legs, and my ass, while not being as tight as it used to be, Ben says it still looks good in jeans. Over all I am pleased with my body. And Ben likes it! So I'm good.

After giving my pubic bush a little maintenance, I stepped into the shower. I took a quick shower, then stepped out and dried myself. Walking nude into the bedroom I sat at my desktop and logged into Marriage Heat. I love being nude so this wasn't unusual. I've even been known to do housework partially clothed or nude when I am alone in the house or sometimes when it is just Ben and I. Of course I don't get much housework done when he is around!

I read several wonderful stories and soon began to feel really aroused as my hand found it's way to my warm moistened pussy. I clicked on one of my favorite stories, "My Backdoor Man" by Ladygarden.

I moaned softly as I thrust three fingers in and out of my horny wet cunt slowly at first then gradually with more vigor as I began to read. It felt oh so good! I imagined it was Ben and I in the story. He loves doggy style; it is by far his favorite sexual position. He feels so good when he is pounding me from the rear like a wild animal. His grunts, groans, and moans of pleasure really get me off, not to mention his big hard dick. I love it!

My breathing became deep and shallow as I continued to pump my fingers into me, my hips humped at my hand. My legs spread wide, my toes curled gripping the rug as I closed my eyes and enjoyed the pleasure I was feeling. I tweaked at my sensitive erect nipples with my other hand then put it to my swollen clitoris and began frigging it in a rapid sweet circular motion as I continued to fuck myself with my other hand.

"Ben! Oh, Ben, baby, if feels so good! So wet!" I panted, then brought my fingers to my mouth and tasted my sweet juices. I then slipped them back in.

Within moments I began to feel my orgasm building inside me. "Yes! Yes! Gonna cum! Cumming! Yes! *Oh, oh, oh*!" I cried as my orgasm exploded. I panted heavily as my body spasmed, trying desperately not to fall from the chair.

I smiled as I gradually began to regain my composure. "I am such a bad girl!" I said with a giggle as I slowly ran my hand over my dripping pussy.

After getting a towel and cleaning myself as

well as the chair, I decided to ask Ladygarden about any advice she may have concerning my upcoming photo shoot. Another dear friend and admin of the site, Blondie, chimed in and gave me a great idea for future use as well with candlelight ambience.

I logged off the computer, and then crawled into bed nude and still tingling from my orgasm. Within minutes I was sound asleep.

The Prep

December 27th

I was awakened from my slumber by the ringing of my cell phone at 7:30 am. It was Ben, who by the way neglected to call me the day before. I guess I can't bitch too much, I mean I could have easily called him.

"Hey, babe! Did I wake you?" He said. It was so good to hear the sound of his sweet voice.

"Yeah, but that's okay! I'll let you get away with it this time I guess. I miss you!" I said as I stretched, then wiped the sleep from my eyes. My head ached a little from all the wine of the previous night.

"Sorry I didn't call you yesterday, but it's been balls to the wall since I got here! I miss you too! Can't talk long, just wanted to check in with you while I have a few minutes. " Ben said. I could barely hear him with all the background noise on his end.

"That's okay! I was wondering however. I can't hear you too well so call me later if you can. I love you!"

"Okay, I love you too! Talk to ya later!"

After a quick shower, I dressed and left for the church. I had a few things to talk over with our minister Brother Mike. After leaving the church I went shopping for some outfits for my photo shoot. I went to Victoria's Secret and a local adult novelty store. I purchased three teddies, black, white and baby blue, fishnet stockings, matching crotchless panties, garters, two baby doll nighties and some new batteries for my vibrator, "Mr. Jolly", a present Ben had gotten me for during his times away. Spent a good bit and kinda hoped it would be worth it in the long run.

I went by Cynthia's to pick up Randy. I visited for about an hour and then Randy and I went to my oldest daughter's apartment and visited with her for a bit. Her boyfriend Trey was out working. Alicia had the day off.

We visited with Alicia for a good while, and then stopped at the grocery store on the way home. The rest of the day and evening was pretty much uneventful from there on. Ben did call and we talked briefly before he had to get back to work.

December 28th

Shelly called me around 10:30 and asked if I would like to meet her at Applebee's for lunch. An invitation I accepted. I met her there around 11:15. We ate and talked somewhat about the shoot.

"Why don't you come by the studio? I do not have another appointment till around 2. We can talk more there. Plus I have some ideas and things I want to show you that you may like," she said as we walked to our cars.

I followed her to her studio and we walked inside.

We talked and she showed me different backgrounds and costumes. A "cowgirl " theme in which I would be wearing a red and white western shirt (unbuttoned of course), with a pair of white chaps, and pink cowboy boots with nothing else. There was of course the French maid outfit, this to go along with the teddies and other stuff I purchased. We then went over lighting (Including candlelight! Thanks, Blondie!).

She was really making me feel more at ease about this whole thing. I finally worked up the courage and asked her how she felt about "spread shots". I stood there expecting her to be shocked and offended and cancel the whole thing or laugh me out of her studio.

She smiled and said, "GG, dear, this is all about you and what you want. I am only there to take the pictures. If you feel comfortable and want to "spread and show" then go for it!

We can even use various cloths to cover some and leave some exposed if you are uncomfortable about showing your whole vag. If anytime during the session you want to open the gates, then feel free, my dear."

I let out a big sigh of relief. I still wasn't sure if I would "spread and show" but I felt more excited than nervous at that time. We visited and talked for another hour or so, and then I headed home.

My son Randy was gone when I got home, so I slipped off my shoes and took a brief nap on the sofa. I awakened about an hour later to the sound of my cell phone ringing. It was my daughter Alicia. She asked if I would like to run to town with her. I told her sure, why not.

"Great! Be there in about twenty minutes!" she said.

I am so grateful that my children still enjoy doing things with their old mom and I cherish those times. They are my joy, my heart and I am proud of each of them. I ran a brush through my hair, put it up in a ponytail, freshened up my make up a bit and waited for her arrival.

Alicia and I had a great time together. It was almost dark when I finally got home. I was tired and my feet hurt. Randy was in his room playing a video game when I told him I was going to take a shower.

The hot water felt so wonderfully relaxing. After my shower I slipped into a pair of gray shorts and a Tennessee Volunteer football jersey. I grabbed my laptop and got into bed. I logged into MH for a few minutes, reading a couple of hot stories, then played some video solitaire.

Sandwiches were on the menu for supper this night as I was just too tired to cook. After eating, Randy and I sat and watched some television. Ben called and we talked for several minutes. It was so good to hear his voice. He told me that he thought he might be home by

New Year's Eve, but New Year's Day seemed more realistic.

"Just make it home to me as soon as you can! I love you and I miss you so," I told him.

"I will. Love and miss you too! Tell the kids Happy New Year for me. Bye, baby," he said and hung up the phone.

It was a little after eleven when I finally decided to call it a night. I told Randy midnight and no later. I headed off to bed. I fell asleep shortly after my head hit the pillow.

December 29th & 30th

Not much happened the next couple of days. Ben called a couple times each day which seemed to make me miss him even more. I grew more excited and, YES, nervous as "photo shoot" day drew nearer. I tried to stay busy and keep my mind off of it the best I could.

New Year's Eve

I got up early and did some much needed house cleaning, something I had been neglecting the last couple of days.

I went to the store and bought a sandwich platter and other snacks such as chips, dip and the like. I also purchased a couple bottles of champagne and a few party favors for later that night. The kids, Cynthia and her bunch, Lisa, Gail, and her husband and I were all going to watch the ball drop on television at my house. Funny, it had started out with just the kids and I, but it had blossomed into a full-fledged party. I just wished Ben would be there.

Everyone began arriving around 7:30. Cynthia and her crew brought some ribs and a bottle of Crown. Kristie brought chips and a bottle of wine. Alicia and Trey brought some desserts and a pot of chicken gumbo that Trey had made. Gail and her bunch brought a case of beer, some finger sandwiches and a pie.

Lisa arrived a little before nine bringing some Buffalo wings and a bottle of Tequila (previously opened). Let me tell ya, we had enough food and adult beverages to do the entire block!

We all had a wonderful time! When the ball finally dropped and the clock struck midnight, I gave each of my kids a big hug and kiss and told them I loved them. Ben called shortly there after and wished everyone a Happy New Year. This made me cry champagne tears of joy.

It was a little after one-o'clock when everyone began leaving for home. I picked up a little, snacked on some finger sandwiches, and then headed for a shower and bed

I went to my bedroom and shut the door. I turned on the light to the bathroom, started my water and undressed. After my shower, I slipped on my short purple nightie, which came to about mid-thigh and crawled into bed. With my head still buzzing from the champagne, I grabbed my laptop and logged into MH and finished a story I had been working on.

I read several stories and not surprisingly began feeling a bit horny. I sure wished Ben were home to make love to me. I read a bit more then decided to masturbate.

I began to run my fingers ever so lightly over my cloth-covered breasts, my nipples rapidly becoming erect. I eased my right breast out from my nightie, moistened a finger with my mouth and traced it over the swollen sensitive bud sending a shiver throughout my body. I imagined it was Ben's tongue flicking at my nipple.

I smiled then slowly removed the nightie and lay nude and exposed on the bed, my body full of sexual tension and longing for release. I continued to manipulate my breasts sending wonderful sensations through my body.

I let my right hand travel lightly down over

my abdomen to my dark brown pubic bush and ran my fingers through it. My fingers grazed over my clit then over my moist cunt lips. Goosebumps rose on my skin. I moaned softly as I slipped first one, then a second finger into my pussy. Slowly I began working my fingers in and out as my left hand continued to tweak my tits.

I began to hump my hips at my hand, my breathing deepened as my pleasure slowly intensified. "So good! *Mm-mm, that feels so good!*" I moaned softly.

As good as my fingers felt I wanted something more, I needed something more. I slipped my fingers from my pussy, then got out of bed and retrieved my vibrator "Mister Jolly". I took my pleasure toy from the shoebox that I kept it in and got back in bed.

I ran my fingers up and down its shaft and kissed the head of that fake cock. I closed my eyes and took it into my mouth and began sucking it as I imagined it was Ben's cock. It wasn't as warm and tasty as Ben, but it satisfied a desire I felt at the time.

I sucked the fake dick for a couple of minutes then I removed it from my mouth. I turned the dial to low and ran it slowly over my breast and around my stiff nipples. The sensation was electric (pardon the pun). With my free hand I slowly manipulated my clitoris. I began to feel like I was on a slow burn and my body seemed to beg for release. It hungered to be fucked by Ben!

I slowly ran my pleasure toy down my body to my very wet pussy. "Oh, feels so, s*o good*!" I whimpered softly as I ran it up and down my swollen cunt lips. My body shivered and twitched slightly as it grazed my clit.

I opened my legs wide then slowly inserted it past my lips.

"Oh my! Mm-mm, yes!" I groaned as I began to work it in and out slowly at first, but I gradually picked up the speed. Within minutes

I felt my orgasm beginning to swell inside as I fucked myself with my joy toy from my dear husband.

My hips bucked wildly at my hand as I pumped the fake dick into me. "Yes, *yes*! I'm cumming! Oh-h-h-oh, yes!" I groaned as I buried my face into my pillow to stifle my orgasmic outburst. I removed my vibrator and cupped my cunt with my hand as my back arched off the bed, then spasmed in sweet release.

I giggled softly as I lay there trying to catch my breath and composure. I got out of bed and retrieved a damp washcloth from the bathroom. I wiped between my legs then cleaned "Mr. Jolly" before putting it away. I slipped my nightie back on then fell into a peaceful sleep.

January 1st, 2014...New Year's Day!

I awakened to the sound of thunder. I slipped out of bed and opened the curtain to the large

window in my bedroom and peered outside. I
for one love the sound of a good steady rain.
It just seems to feel so relaxing and in a way, a
bit romantic.

I stood and watched it rain for a moment,
then headed to the bathroom to relieve my
bladder. My mouth felt dry and the faint taste
of wine lingered. I ran a brush through my
hair, then slipped on my robe and headed to
the kitchen for some coffee and a bite of
breakfast.

After eating a small breakfast and watching
some television, I headed to the bathroom for
a shower and to brush my teeth. On my way,
I stopped and peeked in on my son Randy
sleeping soundly.

After a quick shower, I brushed my teeth and
slipped into my baby blue warm up suit (no
bra or panties). I put my hair up in a ponytail
and made my bed.

It was almost 9am when Ben called and told

me it looked like he would be coming home, but it would probably be later that night, not sure exactly what time. I didn't care as long as he made it home to me. I did miss him so. My son Randy awakened a short time later. He does not share the same views about rainy days as I do as you can imagine.

Since my sweet beloved would be coming home, I began thinking about my upcoming appointment with Shelly and couldn't help but smile. I was still nervous about it, but also excited and looking forward to it. Wanting to keep my secret, I called Shelly and asked her if I could keep my "photo apparel" at her studio.

"Absolutely! Bring 'em over!" She replied.

It was almost noon when I finally left the house. After dropping Randy off at a friend's, I took my stuff to Shelly's studio. She was busy preparing to leave for a shoot, so she showed me where to put my stuff and we spoke briefly before she had to leave.

After leaving Shelly's, I drove over to the salon and visited with Gail and the girls, as well as a couple of my former clients. We had a nice visit and to be honest I kinda missed working there… the atmosphere, the camaraderie, and the meeting of new people. That being said, I do enjoy my life now a bit more.

It was around 2:30 when I left the salon and headed to the grocery store to pick up a few things we needed. The cashier who checked me out was kind of grouchy and rude, rolling her eyes at me when I told her that she had over charged me on a of couple items. This irritated me and I had to bite my tongue to keep from giving her a piece of my mind. Thank you, dear Lord, for helping me control my temper!

The rain had stopped by the time I made it home. I unloaded the groceries and put them away before fixing myself a sandwich and sat down to eat. After eating I put my favorite Bob Seager CD into the stereo and cranked it up as I piddled around with some housework.

Later that evening, I cooked Randy and I some supper and settled in in front of the TV. Randy didn't eat much since he had eaten pizza earlier with a friend. I lay on the sofa while he went to his room to play on his XBox.

I guess I must have dozed off because the next thing I knew it was after 9pm. I thought of Ben and though he said it may be later that night before he would make it home, I couldn't help but wonder if he would be able to make it home that night at all. I missed my man and wanted him home, but not at the risk of him falling asleep at the wheel depending on when he was able to leave.

It was almost 10pm when I showered and readied for bed. After telling Randy not to stay up any later than eleven. I crawled into bed and began reading a book I had purchased a couple days prior. It was around 12:30 when I heard the front door shut.

I quickly got out of bed and walked to the living room. There standing at the door was my handsome man looking tired. He smiled when he saw me and I attacked him, almost knocking him down as I leapt into his strong arms.

It felt so good to feel his arms around me as we kissed. His lips felt so warm against mine as I welcomed his sweet tongue into my mouth. I had so missed this and could feel my cunt becoming quite moist.

"Baby, I have missed you so much! So glad you are finally home! I love you!" I said as I gazed into his deep brown eyes.

He grinned, then said, "I missed you too, baby! I love you too! Is Randy asleep?"

We kissed again, before I could pull back and I say, "He's in bed. Yeah, he is asleep. You look tired, my baby! Why don't you go take a shower? Would you like for me to fix you a drink? Are you hungry?" I asked.

"It was a long ride. Yeah, a drink sounds good. Not really hungry though," he said as he headed for our bedroom, pulling his luggage behind him.

I fixed him a Seagrams and 7 over ice, flipped off the lights then headed to our room. He was standing in the bathroom, his shirt off and was unfastening his jeans when I walked in.

"Here, baby, let me help you with that!" I said with a smile and a wink as I handed him his drink.

I kissed him and pulled gently on his bottom lip with my teeth as my hands worked to finish unfastening his jeans, slowly unzipping them. I kissed him again as I slowly pushed his jeans down over his hips. Much to my delight he wasn't wearing any underwear.

I smiled as I slowly dropped to my knees and finished pulling his jeans down until he was finally able to step out of them. His long thick flaccid cock and large balls hung before my eyes in their magnificent glory.

I looked up at him and gave him a mischievous grin then taking his limp meat into my hand, I softly kissed the head. I ran my tongue teasingly over the slit, and then bathed the head with my tongue.

"Baby! Oh man, it is good to be home!" He groaned as his cock began to thicken.

I glanced up at him and took him into my mouth. His scent filling my nostrils as my pussy became wet with desire. I continued to suck his dick, feeling it grow firmer as I held and fondled his balls with my right hand.

Ben groaned and slowly began thrusting his hips, literally fucking my throat. I gagged a couple times but was loving every second of it.

I pulled back and began to concentrate on the head, giving it a good going over with my tongue. I love sucking his cock and tasting him so it was making me so aroused. I moaned softly as I feasted on him.

Ben's body twitched and his knees seemed to buckle a bit as he said, "So good! Gina, baby! *Oh-h-h, baby! I'm gonna cum! I'm gonna cum, mm-mph!"*

I held him in my mouth as he spasmed with his climax; his warm semen filled my mouth and coated my throat. It was a big load, but I managed to swallow it with little problem.

I gave his cock a gentle kiss, then stood, kissing my way up his body. I put my arms around him, grabbing his butt with both hands. We kissed, the taste of his cum still lingering in my mouth.

"Take your shower, baby, then come to bed. I will be waiting," I whispered softly into his ear.

I walked back into the bedroom and gently

shut our bedroom door. Removing my clothes, I slipped into bed nude and awaited his arrival. I opened my legs and ran my hand over my hot dripping cunt and slowly began to finger myself as I waited. I considered going ahead and giving myself the release my body ached for, but I held back.

I still had my hand on my cunt, when Ben emerged from the bathroom. We both gave a smile as he walked over to the bed and got in.

"Did you cum, baby?" he asked then kissed me.

"No, I wanted to wait for you! I've missed you so much!" I replied and kissed him with a heated passion.

He smiled and began loving on my breast, flicking his tongue ever so teasingly at my sensitive hardened nipples. He suckled on each one.

"Mm-mm, baby! You're driving me insane!" I

groaned as he gently nipped at my buds with his teeth. I have never climaxed just by him loving my tits, but if he would have lingered over them much longer, I believe I would have.

He began slowly kissing his way down my body, raising goose bumps on my skin.

"You have such a pretty pussy, baby! Such a thick bush, I love it!" He said as he ran his fingers through my pubic garden.

"*Baby! Oh-Ah! I'm...oh-oh-oh!*" I cried as he slipped a finger into me, pushing me over the edge as I exploded in orgasm. I panted heavily as my body lurched, my hips rose off the bed.

"So beautiful! I love watching you cum! I must have a taste!" he said, and put his sweet lips to my cunt and kissed its swollen wet lips.

"*Oh, yeah! Baby!*" I panted, my body twitched as I felt his tongue run along my cunt lips as he lapped up my juices. I do so love how my loving husband eats me.

I was delirious with pleasure as he continued to eat me out with such fervor. Within moments I began to cum again.

"Cumming! Oh-0h-oh-*oh, baby!*" I groaned as my body writhed. I held his head in place with my hand as I fed him more of my sweet juices.

He kissed his way back up my trembling body. We kissed, our tongues entwined passionately.

"I love you, Gina," he said softly as he slowly stroked his now semi-erect penis.

"I love you too, my dear man!" I replied, reaching and placing my hand on his as he jacked himself. "Baby, Why don't you lay back?" I told him and then softly kissed his sweet lips.

He turned onto his back, his hand still slowly pumping his cock.

"Let me take care of that for you, baby!" I whispered, while kissing him once more.

I kissed his chest, swirling my tongue over his nipples. I ran my tongue down his torso, teasingly flicking my tongue in and around his naval.

I grasped his dick in my hand and just held it, loving the way it felt. I gazed upon it, admiring its size as I gave it a couple of slow strokes. I so love his cock!

Such power it has over me and my body; this wonderful organ had impregnated me three times. It had given me such pleasure and countless orgasms over the years (not to mention the pleasure it had given him) and I thank the Lord for the blessing of marital sex.

I leaned forward and licked the pre-cum that had formed on the tip. I then took his dickhead into my mouth and bathed it with my tongue as I began to suck on it. Needless to say he was rock hard almost instantly.

I took him deep into my throat and held him there just for a moment, and slowly moved back up until I let it escape my lips.

I smiled at him as I straddled him. I longed to feel him inside me. No, I needed to feel him inside me. I could see by the look on his face that he desperately wanted the same thing.

Holding his hard-on with one hand, I slowly lowered myself upon him. I gasped as he penetrated me. His cock stretched me as I impaled myself until he was buried balls' deep inside my hungry cunt.

"Baby, you feel so good! I love you so much! I've missed you so much!" I panted as I began riding him. "I need to be fucked, baby! Does my pussy feel good, baby?"

"Feels so good, baby! Ride my cock! Yeah! Your pussy is so wet and tight!" Ben groaned as he thrust his hips up to meet mine, his pubic bone bumped and rubbed against my clit so deliciously.

"Mm-mph! So good! Baby! Baby! I'm gonna cum! Oh-oh, fuck me! I'm cumming!" I cried. I collapsed on top of him. My body trembled as my cunt pulsed around his dick.

Once I regained my composure I slowly began to ride him again. "I'm gonna fuck your balls off, baby! I'm gonna make you cum as hard as you just made me! Did you miss this pussy, baby? I definitely missed your big dick! I played with myself thinking about fucking you, baby!" I panted as I watched the expressions of lust in his face and eyes.

He grunted and groaned, holding my hips with his hands as he thrust up hard into me.

"Mm-mph! Mm-mph! YES! YES! That's it! Fuck me! Tell me when you're gonna cum, baby! I wanna see it! I want to watch you shoot off, okay, baby?" I panted as I humped him hard.

"Fuck me, Gina! Oh-h-h, now! Oh, shit!" he groaned.

I lifted off of him just in time to see the first spurt of his cum fountain. I sat back on his thighs and grasped his throbbing member with my hand and pumped it, milking his cum from his balls onto his pubes and stomach.

"So, so hot!" I panted as I put my hand to my cunt and "jilled" off my clit as he watched. I came then collapsed beside him. "I love you, my baby. Welcome home!" I giggled as I lay in his arms and kissed him softly on his lips.

He smiled. "I love you too, baby, but I believe I could use a damp rag or something."

We both laughed, then I got out of bed and retrieved a damp rag from the bathroom and cleaned the semen puddles from his stomach and pubic area.

We lay together nude and cuddled, before finally drifting asleep a little before 3 am.

January 2nd, the rest of the day

Ben was still sleeping peacefully when I eased out of bed. I couldn't help but smile as I looked upon his sleeping frame. It was then that I realized I had neglected to close the curtain to our large bedroom window last night.

Still nude I walked over and closed them. I couldn't help but laugh about it. The area the window looked out over was fenced in and pretty private, so I wasn't concerned too much about someone seeing anything. Still the exhibitionist side of me did feel a bit of a thrill.

I went to the bathroom and slipped on a pair of jeans and a shirt. I gently opened the bedroom door and headed for the kitchen. My son Randy was sitting at the kitchen table eating a bowl of cereal.

"Hey, babe! How long have you been up?" I asked as I began fixing a pot of coffee.

"Not long. Is dad home?" Randy asked.

"Sure is! Got home late last night. He's sleeping so try and keep the noise down, okay?" I said with a yawn.

"Thought so, saw his boots by the door. Can I go four wheeler riding?" he asked as he finished his cereal.

"Sure, just be careful and make your bed before you leave!" I replied.

When Randy left, I watched a little television. Afterward I called my parents. I hadn't talked to them since Christmas.

My dad answered the phone and I talked with him for a couple minutes. He is not much of a conversationalist on the phone, saying just what he has to say then abruptly handing the phone off to my mom.

I love talking to my mom. She can be such a card sometimes. She has such a dry sense of humor and is smart as a whip. She is a devoted Christian, with a deep love for the

Lord and her family. She is my hero! We talked for a good twenty minutes before finally hanging up.

It was almost 11am when Ben finally awakened, walking into the kitchen clad only in his boxers.

"Well good morning, my love! How did you sleep last night? " I said with a smile as I gave a quick wink.

He chuckled and replied, "I slept pretty good actually. How long have you been up?"

"A couple hours. Are you hungry? " I asked.

"Yeah, I could go for a bite! Randy still asleep?" he asked.

"No, he's gone on his four wheeler," I said as I cooked him some eggs, sausage and toast.

We made a little small talk as he ate. When he finished, he went to take a shower (alone). I did some laundry and picked up a bit.

Shelly called around one to confirm whether we were still on for the shoot.

"Sure, I'd love to get together tomorrow, Shell, that would be great!" I said, playing it off as if it was nothing, as Ben was standing not far from me.

A knot formed in my stomach as the realization hit that the shoot was the next day. Ben was on the couch watching TV and a smile instantly crossed my lips.

We decided to go see our girls. They were both at work, but Ben hadn't seen or talked to them since Christmas day. Randy stayed home as he and a couple friends were riding four wheelers.

After visiting with Alicia and Kristie for a bit, Ben and I went to the Golden Corral and ate. We then went to the Home Depot to get a couple new batteries for his drill.

It was around 4:30 or 5pm when we finally made it home. He checked and cleaned out his truck as I fixed a little something for supper. We ate around 6:30.

After supper we watched some TV together. It was almost 8 when Ben went to take his shower. It was back to work for him in the morning and 4am would come early.

It was also back to school for Randy as well as I shuttled him off for his shower. I picked up the kitchen and put some clothes in the dryer. Seems to be an endless supply of dirty clothes at our house!

Randy seemed to want to take his time going to bed, but after threatening to get his dad on his ass about it he quickly complied.

I walked to our bedroom where Ben was already in bed. I walked over and kissed his sweet lips. "I love you, my sweet man!" I said, then kissed him again, this time slipping my tongue into his mouth and moaning softly.

"I love you too! Are you coming to bed?" he asked.

"I'm gonna read for a few minutes, then I will be. Get some sleep, my baby!" I said softly and kissed him once more.

I went into the living room and sat on the sofa and read the book I'd been reading. I read for about an hour, then went and took a quiet quick shower.

After my shower, I slipped into my gown and got into bed, snuggling close to my sleeping warm naked husband. I fell asleep smiling.

The Shoot

January 3rd ... Photo Day!

I was rudely awakened by the alarm clock at 6:15am. Ben had long since left for work. I didn't even hear him get up, much less leave. Usually, I awaken to him getting up or rustling around getting dressed, or he wakes me wanting a piece of pussy, but not on this morning.

I lay in bed trying to wake up, when it came to me what day it was. It was the day of my photo shoot. I giggled nervously as the butterflies returned to flutter in my stomach.

I lay in bed for a few minutes. My mind was racing, a mental war went on about if I should go through with it, or chicken out and call Shelly cancelling the whole thing.

I finally got out of bed, slipped on a robe and got Randy up for school. It seemed a bit redundant to go back to school at the end of the week, if you asked me. Which they didn't!

He was remarkably easy to get up, which was unusual. I fixed Randy and I a quick breakfast and off he went to catch the bus.

After he left, I settled on the couch to do some reading. I was hoping it would calm my nerves and take my mind off a few things. No such luck! All I could think about was my pending photo shoot with Shelly.

I decided to busy myself with housework. I put away dishes, washed, dried and put away three loads of clothes. I mopped, made beds and even cleaned out my car. Before I knew it, it was after eleven o'clock.

It was around noon, when Cynthia called. We talked for a good half hour, mainly about my photo shoot. Actually, talking to her about it seemed to help my nerves. Keeping the secret meant keeping my feelings and anxiety bottled up inside. I was able to release a lot of that talking to her.

A little after two Shelly called to once again verify that it was still on. I told her it was, though I was scared out of my wits. She laughed and said, "GG, you will do great! Just be yourself and remember why and who you're doing it for. We will take it at your own pace girl. Nothing to be nervous about!"

After hanging up with Shelly, I went and took a nice hot bath.

As I lay in the tub I began to think about Ben and how much I loved him. All I needed to do was do as Ladygarden on Marriage Heat and Shelly my photographer had advised: just keep my mind focused on him.

My mind did focus on him and my fingers found their way to my cunt. I closed my eyes as I slowly stroked my love bud. In a few short minutes my body was overcome with my orgasm, taking my breath as my body trembled.

After my bath, I dried myself and walked

nude into my bedroom. I stood at my closet trying to figure out what to wear. I laughed and thought to myself, "What difference does it make! I'm just gonna take them off anyway!"

I decided to wear a pink sweatshirt that had "Love Pink" written in white letters across the front. No bra.

I slipped on a pink laced thong and some designer jeans that fit a little tight, but not " trashy" tight and a pair of black sandal top heels (think they may fit into the "Fuck-me pumps" category. Hehe!)

I left Randy a note telling him I was going to see my friend, Shelly, and shouldn't be gone too long. I then called and left a message on Ben's phone telling him in case he got home before me.

I arrived at Shelly's studio just as she was closing up. She met me at the door. "Hey, girl! Come on in. Let me finish closing and I will be with you in a sec. I got a bottle of Brandy if you want to fix yourself something to drink," she said.

"I think I will, thanks. Do you want one?" I asked.

"Sure, I will take one!" she replied.

We talked for several minutes about husbands, kids and just life in general. Brandy was new to me, as I have never really drunk it before. After two glasses, I had a nice little buzz. Not drunk, just that warm little feeling.

"Wait right here, I will be right back!" she said, and walked to the back.

I sipped on my drink and I heard her call me, "Hey, GG! Come back here for a second!"

I walked to the back and saw her standing and holding her camera. She then snapped a picture. This caught me completely off guard.

"Gotta start somewhere and you look adorable in that outfit. Why don't you turn around for me?" she asked as she snapped another picture.

I became really tense at that point, but did as she requested, hearing the camera click a couple more times as I did.

"Wonderful! OK, Why don't you bend over just a bit, put your hands on your knees!" she said.

I did and could feel my face heat up from blushing. I was still nervous and tense but also began feeling kinda sexy.

"Beautiful! Listen, I just want you to have fun with this. Just relax and be yourself. Okay? Now why don't you unfasten your jeans a bit and raise your shirt and show your abdomen," she said, sensing my nervousness.

I did as the camera clicked again, then again.

"Great job! Are you wearing a bra?" She asked.

"No." I answered.

"Perfect! Go ahead and raise your shirt a bit higher, just to where it shows the bottom of your breasts! Awesome! " she applauded as she clicked another photo.

I remembered the advice Ladygarden had given me about focusing on Ben and the reason I was doing this: My love for him.

I soon began to relax.

A smile crossed my lips as I propped my foot on a chair and removed one shoe, then another. I'm not sure if the smile was because of my thoughts of Ben, the fact that I felt extremely sexy or a combination of both.

With my left leg still propped up on the chair, I raised my shirt and exposed my right breast. The camera clicked. I began to feel my nervousness begin to melt away.

I sat in the chair and slowly began to remove my shirt until my breasts were fully exposed. I could hear the camera clicking away as I cupped my tits with my hands. My nipples were becoming hard from the excitement of the moment.

"Very nice! Roll with it, girl!" Shelly said as she clicked a couple more shots.

I stood and ever so slowly began removing my jeans, exposing my pink-laced thong.

"Very nice! Why don't you turn around and take them off!" Shelly said.

I smiled then turned my back to her as I began pushing the jeans over my hips, then bent over as I pushed them down to my ankles giving her a full ass shot. The camera clicked away.

She took several pictures of me in just my

thong before having to stop and reload some more film. "GG, Why don't you slip into one of those teddies while I load up and adjust the lights," Shelly suggested.

I decided on the white one. I slipped off my thong. I put on the white crotch-less panties, garters, and teddy. My face heated with an excited blush as for the first time my full bush would be exposed.

"Very sexy! You rock that outfit girl! " Shelly said with a smile as she adjusted the lights to a soft amber.

She began taking pictures of me from every angle, from standing to lying on the cloth-covered platform (no spread shots yet). We did the same with the blue teddy as well as the black. With the black teddy, she had me put my heels back on. She adjusted the tint of the lighting with each one to give maximum effect.

Next came the "cowgirl" theme. Red and

white western shirt unbuttoned with white chaps, white crotch-less panties, pink cowboy hat and pink boots. She even produced a bullwhip as a prop. Behind me she put up a western prairie scene depicting buffaloes, Indians, and of course cowboys. This was really fun!

Next came the hardhat, black teddy with black crotch-less panties, and tool belt. She even had me hold a large pipe wrench. Seeing as how Ben works in the oilfield business, she felt he would appreciate it.

The shoot seemed to move along at a rapid pace as we moved to the baby doll nightie. Shelly was very professional and instructed me on poses she felt would look good. Though she said she had never done this type of shoot before, you could have fooled me.

"Feel like doing some nudes now, GG?" Shelly asked as she reloaded her camera once again.

"Sure. Can we use candlelight for these?" I replied as I removed the nightie and stood completely nude and exposed.

"One ahead of ya, dear! You have a really nice body, GG! Ben is gonna love this I guarantee it!" she replied as she began setting candles in strategic locations, then lighting them.

"Shall we begin, hon?" she said with a smile as she turned the lights down to soft amber that accentuated the glow from the candlelight.

My nipples were hard as I cupped my breasts with my hands and rolled my buds between my fingers as her camera clicked away. I felt so beautiful and sexy at that moment, no nervousness or shyness whatsoever. It felt so erotic with the candlelight and the warmth of her studio lights (You were so right Ladygarden and Blondie!). I could feel my cunt becoming moist. How could it not!

She took several standing frontal shots of me, rear shots both standing and slightly bent over capturing me from every angle.

She put several throw pillows down on the dark cloth covered platform and said, "Why don't you lay down and let's get some shots!"

I smiled as I walked slowly to the platform and lay upon it, amongst the throw pillows. Shelly clicked away with her camera as she gave instructions on various poses: On my back with hands over my head. On my back with my hands holding my breasts. On my stomach, on my side, on my hands and knees with my hand covering my pussy.

I felt so sexy and beautiful. My nervousness was gone as I kept my mind on my dear Ben. I am not gonna lie, I was terribly aroused. My nipples were rock hard, and, yes, my cunt was quite moist.

I decided to go for a spread shot. I sat up and put my legs in front of me and opened wide. I felt my face grow very warm, not sure if it was from the lights or if I was blushing. I simply cannot explain the feelings and thoughts that ran through my mind. All I know is… I felt really good about myself, my body, and my love for my dear Ben.

Shelly's camera continued to click away as I lay on my back, keeping my legs spread. I ran my hand down to my bush and ran my fingers through it, then ran my hands over my inner thighs. I cupped my pussy with one hand as I got lost in my thoughts of my loving husband.

What happened next, was almost like a dream. I hadn't planned it, but I did it. I slipped a finger into my pussy. It was only for a moment, but as I later found out, Shelly captured that moment.

She took a few more shots finishing out the roll of film. We decided to call it a wrap.

"Great job, girl! See? It wasn't so bad now was it? I think we got some great shots!" Shelly said, as I began to dress.

It was done. I had done it! I wanted to jump up and down in celebration. I managed to control my emotions as I said, "Thank you, Shelly! Thank you so much for agreeing to do this! I really appreciate it."

"Not a problem, GG! Think I have something new to add to my resume," she laughed. "I should have your photos ready Tuesday. Might have them ready Monday, but more than likely Tuesday."

"Sounds great, Shell," I said as I finished dressing and put my other garments back into the bag. I hugged her neck, then left for my car.

On the drive home, my joy came out in laughter. I was so proud of myself for going through with it. I was also extremely horny and couldn't wait to get home and jump my dear husband's bones. I put a Bruce Springsteen CD in, "Born to Run" and cranked it up. I was home in no time.

I was a bit disappointed to see Ben's truck wasn't home yet, but it was early. As I walked into the house, I found a note from Randy. He had gone to a friend's house to play a new game his friend had purchased.

I walked into my and Ben's bedroom and placed the bag of garments into my closet. I then took off my shoes and put them into the closet.

I unbuttoned my jeans, then walked over and shut the bedroom door. I unzipped my jeans and slipped them off, then took off my sweatshirt. Clad only in my lace thong and bra, I walked into the bathroom and put my hair in a ponytail as I looked into the large lavatory mirror.

"So proud of you! You are one crazy girl! Horny, but crazy none the less!" I told the middle-aged woman looking back at me in the mirror.

I continued to look at myself in the mirror as

I cupped my breasts with both hands.

"Got some nice tits, if I do say so myself!" I told my reflection as I massaged my bra covered breasts.

I grinned as I unclasped my lace bra and ever so slowly removed it, exposing one breast at a time. My nipples were rock hard as they came into view. I let out a soft moan as I gently tweaked each one.

I so wished Ben would have been home, but he wasn't and I needed to get off. I looked into the mirror and giggled. "Well, babe, guess it's me and you! Wanna make love?" I said, then laughed feeling a little silly and very horny.

I left the bathroom and walked back into the bedroom clad only in my lace thong, the crotch was already quite damp. I lay across the bed and began to manipulate my breasts and nipples. The sensations I felt were so delicious and sent erotic messages to my horny wet cunt.

My body felt like it was going to explode if I didn't cum soon. I let my hand drift to my cloth-covered pussy and cupped it. I began to rub the full length of my cunt. The combination of my hand and the friction of the cloth on my clit soon sent me into a "cumtastic" explosion.

"Oh, oh! I'm cumming! Oh-ah!" I cried as my body tensed and contracted on the bed as my right hand cupped my cunt and my left squeezed my left tit.

As I lay there enjoying the afterglow of my orgasm, I brought my fingers up to my mouth and tasted my pussy juices. I love the taste of my juices, whether it is from my fingers or from Ben's dick after we fuck. His cum mixed with mine tastes so exquisite.

As a friend of mine once said, the great thing about being a girl is our ability to have multiple orgasms, and I wanted more.

I closed my eyes and began to picture Ben lying in bed, his dick hard and throbbing waiting to be engulfed by my wet pussy as he slowly stroked himself, teasing me. I once again began to touch myself.

"Fuck me! Oh, baby!" I panted as I thrust my fingers rapidly in and out of my pussy feeling another orgasm building inside.

"Oh, oh, ah-h!" I squealed as I spasmed once more, my breath leaving my lungs.

I lay there gasping for breath as my second orgasm subsided. I got out of bed and my legs quivered as I reached under the bed and removed the shoebox that I kept my "Mr. Jolly " in. I took him out and crawled back in bed.

I spread my legs wide and ran my hands over the damp curls of my pubic bush and swollen wet pussy lips. My body twitched as my fingers grazed my sensitive swollen clit as I gently stroked it. A low groan escaped my lips as I turned Mr. Jolly on low speed, then put it between my thighs and ran the vibrating phallus over my entire cunt.

"Oh, oh, oh, ah, baby! Oh, Yes-s-s-s! Give it to me! Give me some dick! Oh, BEN, Baby!" I panted as I slowly inserted my pleasure toy into my throbbing cunt, slowly working it in and out. My eyes closed as I imagined it was my dear Ben's dick inside me giving me such pleasure.

I worked my hips in rhythm to my thrusting hand as I continued to fuck myself with the fake cock until I felt my third orgasm beginning to swell deep inside me. I was panting heavily then my body lurched and my hips rose off the bed as I began to cum once more. "Oh-ah!" I groaned unable to form any words for my pleasure. I left my toy inside me, turning off the vibrations as my body calmed, my pussy pulsing around it.

I lay there for several minutes with Mr. Jolly stuffed inside my cunt, flexing my pussy muscles around it. I was delirious with pleasure as I reached between my legs once more.

I slowly began to work that wonderful pleasure toy in and out of my now sloppy, wet cunt.

"Mm-mm, feels so good!" I panted as I humped my hips while I thrust the toy dick into me. *"Pump it, Pump that pussy!"* I groaned, as I turned the vibrations on to low. My body shivered as I grabbed a pillow and hugged it next to me with my free hand, biting a corner as I turned the vibrations up a notch to medium. The pleasure was too intense and more than I could handle as another orgasm began to swell inside me.

"Oh! Oh, YES! YES! Gonna… gonna cum! Oh, Ben, baby, I'm cumming!" I squealed as I began to cum. I thrashed around on the bed.

After I'd recovered I walked to the bathroom and started a shower.

Feeling refreshed from the shower, I slipped on a pair of blue jean cut-offs and a dark blue t-shirt. It was about then that I heard Randy call for me. I walked into the kitchen and began preparing supper.

Randy and I were about finished eating when Ben walked through the door. He walked over and kissed me, then fixed himself a plate. We sat and talked about his day as he ate.

"How was your day?" he asked me, taking a drink from his tea.

"It was good. Shelly and I had a good visit," I said as my heart beat a little faster, knowing the secret I was keeping.

"That's good. How was she doing?" He asked.

"She's doing good. Are you still off tomorrow?" I asked as I got up and rinsed out my plate, then began emptying out the dishwasher.

"Yeah, told Glen I may stop by and help him work on his deck he is building sometime tomorrow. Unless you had something you wanted to do?" He replied.

"That's fine, baby. No, I don't have anything special planned. May go by the salon and see if Gail wants to have lunch. Kristie mentioned something about coming by sometime in the morning. Wants me to do her hair. Decided she wants to lighten it up a bit," I said as I began to clean the kitchen.

"OK." Ben turned his attention to Randy. "Hey, sport, wanna go with me tomorrow? Thought we could go by and check on a new seat for your four-wheeler? Besides I'm sure Glen would appreciate the extra help."

"Yes, sir, I guess," Randy replied.

Randy and Ben helped me finish cleaning the kitchen then Ben went to take his shower. I sent Randy off to take his as well.

The three of us then sat in the living room. Ben and Randy watched television, while I read my book.

It was a little after eleven when I sent a sleepy Randy off to bed. He had been dozing off now and then on the sofa. Ben and I sat up a bit longer, both enjoying a glass of wine before heading to bed.

Ben clicked off the lights and we headed for bed. Ben gently shut our bedroom door behind us. I took off my clothes and slipped on a gown, then headed to the bathroom to pee.

As I was sitting on the pot, Ben walked in nude and began brushing his teeth. I sat and just admired his muscular nude frame. My eyes seemed to linger to the sight of his beautiful cock and large balls.

I wiped myself, then stood and made my way past him, pinching him playfully on the right butt cheek.

"Hey! Watch that!" he exclaimed as he finished rinsing his mouth.

I giggled as I picked up my toothbrush and began brushing my teeth.

"Oh, you find that amusing?" he asked, then playfully smacked me across the ass. I squealed and turned. I threatened him with my toothbrush (Really scaring him! Yeah, right!).

As I bent forward to rinse my mouth, I felt Ben's hands on my hips. "Stay just like you are, baby!" he said as I attempted to raise myself up.

I glanced back and smiled at him as his hands pushed my gown up to my waist, exposing my naked ass. I let out a soft moan as his hands ran over and massaged the globes of my ass.

"Someone had a bit of fun earlier, didn't she?" he said softly.

"What are you talking about, baby?" I groaned as he groped my ass.

"Some naughty girl left her sex toy on the floor and the bed is a mess!" he replied.

"I was just... Oh, BEN, oh, baby!" I groaned as he suddenly slipped his thumb into my asshole.

"Did you cum hard while you fucked yourself with that fake cock, baby? Did you? My naughty girl," he said, looking at me through the mirror.

"Oh, YES, I did, baby! I was so naughty! I came four times, baby, thinking about you fucking me!" I said, propping myself with my hands as I looked back at him through the mirror.

"Is that what you want? Would you like for me to fuck you? Say it, baby, tell me what you want, you naughty girl!" Ben said, reaching forward with one hand and grasping one of my breasts.

"YES, baby! Fuck me! Fuck me now!" I said as I reached between my legs and began fingering my clit. My pussy became really moist rather quickly.

"Oh, Ben! YES! *Oh-h, yes!*" I groaned as I felt the swollen head of his dick slip past my moist cunt lips as he pushed deep into me.

Through the mirror we looked at one another as he took me from behind. His hands held my hips as he pounded into me.

"Is this what you want, baby? You want to be fucked? You like to fuck, don't you my naughty girl!" Ben growled as he pumped hard and deep.

"Y-yes, f-fuck m-me! Oh, Ben, don't stop! Mmph! Oh, oh, baby!" I panted, rapidly stroking my clit with my fingers as he stroked his big dick in and out of my hot pussy.

"Your pussy feels so tight, baby! Feels so good!" Ben groaned, grabbing a handful of my hair as he fucked me from behind.

I began to feel my orgasm approaching, my fifth of the evening.

"I'm cumming! Baby, I-I'm c-c-cumming! Oh, yeah!" I exclaimed, my body tensed and my legs trembled beneath me.

Ben continued to pump me for several minutes before finally exploding inside me with a deep groan.

We stayed with him buried deep inside me, a bit of his cum oozed out of me. We kissed as he slipped from me. After cleaning ourselves we headed for bed.

We said a brief prayer together and I snuggled into his arms.

"I love you, my man!" I whispered and I kissed his lips.

"I love you too, my naughty girl," he murmured. We then drifted off to sleep.

The Reveal

Saturday, January 4th

I awakened a little before 9. Ben wasn't in bed. I stretched, then got out of bed and walked to the bathroom for the morning ritual pee. After doing my business, I walked back into the bedroom where I noticed my vibrator "Mr. Jolly " laying on the floor next to the bed. I couldn't help but smile as I walked over and picked it up.

"Oh, the wonderful trouble you got me into! Thank you," I whispered and giggled as I walked back to the bathroom and cleaned it, before putting it back in its proper place under the bed.

I opened the bedroom door and made my way to the kitchen. On the table was a note from Ben:

Good morning! Gone to Glen's, be back later on! Fresh coffee is made. Love you!

Ben and Randy

I made a couple pieces of toast, then poured myself a cup of coffee. After eating and having another cup of coffee, I headed to the bathroom for a shower, after which I slipped on a blue thong, a pair of jeans and a purple button up shirt with a white camisole underneath. It was almost 10 when Kristie called and said she was on her way.

"Okay, babe! Have you eaten?" I asked.

"No, but I am going to pick something up on the way. Want me to pick you up anything?" she asked.

"I don't believe so, thank you anyway! I just ate a bite." I replied.

After hanging up the phone, I picked up a little as I awaited Kristie's arrival. She came a short time later carrying a large fountain drink and a bag with the stuff for her hair. We visited and I did her hair, which turned out really cute. She and I hung out, just lounging around the house till around 2.

After she left, I loaded up and drove over to the salon. They were pretty busy so I offered my assistance and washed the hair of three customers. Once business thinned out a bit, Gail, the other girls and I had a nice visit. I stayed till almost 4:30 then headed for home.

The rest of the day was pretty uneventful, just a quiet Saturday. Ben took us out to eat fish for supper that evening, then we watched a movie at home before calling it a night.

Sunday, January 5th

I was awakened around 5:30am by the sound of Ben rummaging around in the bathroom. I got out of bed and walked to the bathroom and found him standing in his jeans and no shirt, obviously looking for something.

"Morning, babe! What are you looking for?" I asked, planting a soft kiss on his cheek.

"Looking for my deodorant, have you seen it by any chance?" he said.

"Yeah, I put it in the linen closet behind you.

Things were getting a little cluttered so I put some stuff in there." I said as I left the bathroom and headed back to bed.

"Thanks! I knew I hadn't run out. Are you and Randy going to church this morning?" Ben asked as he walked into the bedroom, slipping his shirt on.

"Yeah, Kristie and I are gonna work the nursery." I replied as I grabbed my laptop.

"'K. Well, tell Brother Mike that I am going to mow the church grounds Thursday. I will be off that day." Ben said as he buttoned his shirt then slipped on his boots.

"Okay, I will. What would you like to eat this evening? Anything in particular?" I asked.

"Doesn't matter to me, baby. Well, I gotta go! See y'all this evening. I love you." he said, then walked over and kissed my lips.

"Love you too! Be careful." I said as he left.

I piddled around on the computer for a bit then headed for a shower. After a nice shower I slipped on my new blue Terry cloth robe and walked to the kitchen to fix some breakfast. It was around 8 when I awakened Randy. We ate then I went to get dressed as did Randy.

We left for church a little after nine (Church starts at 10). Kristie was already there when we arrived. Church went really well. Kristie and I had 7 little ones to entertain. All of them behaved really well for the most part. After church I talked to Brother Mike about what Ben had said and about some upcoming church events. It was almost noon when we finally left and I asked Kristie if she would like to go with Randy and myself to get something to eat. She agreed and came along as we went and ate at a local restaurant.

After eating Randy and I drove to Cynthia's and visited with her and her bunch for a couple hours before heading home a little before four. When we arrived home I was a bit surprise to see Ben's truck sitting in the driveway. Pleasantly surprised! He was sitting at the kitchen table drinking a beer when we walked into the house.

"Hey, baby! What are you doing home? Didn't expect you till a bit later." I said as I walked over and gave him a kiss.

"Took off early. Gonna probably have to work over night tomorrow, so I called it a day." he answered, then took another swallow from his beer.

"I see. What time you going in tomorrow?" I asked as I slipped off my shoes.

"Probably around 2 or so. What have you two been up to? How was church?" Ben asked.

"It was good. I told Brother Mike what you said. He said that would be fine. We went to eat with Kristie, then Randy and I stopped and visited with Cynthia for a bit." I replied, as I poured myself a glass of wine. "

I bought some steaks, thought I might grill 'em up! What do you think?" Ben asked as he grabbed another beer from the fridge.

"Sounds great, baby," I replied.

It was just before 6 when Ben began grilling the steaks. I worked on fixing some sides, mac and cheese, corn, green beans and the like. It was near 7:30pm when we finally sat down to eat. The steaks were awesome!

After eating, we all sat down and watched TV. After a few minutes, Randy left to go play video games. Ben watched TV for a while as I read a book.

"Well, think I'm gonna go get my shower!" Ben said, rising from the couch and unbuttoning his shirt.

"Okay, babe!" I said looking up from my book and giving him a smile.

"You about ready for bed?" he asked as he walked towards our bedroom.

"Yeah, just gonna finish this chapter and I will be." I replied.

It was after ten when I finally put my book down. Turning off the TV and the lights, I headed for bed. Stopping at Randy's room for a moment to tell him it was time to shut it down, I walked into our room and gently shut the door.

Ben was in bed watching TV and he gave me a slight grin. I slipped off my shirt as I made my way to the bathroom giving him a quick wink. I walked into the bathroom and started my shower water. I unfastened my skirt making sure my reflection showed in the mirror so Ben could see. I slowly slid the skirt down, bending over as I pushed them down. Dressed only in my thong I made sure Ben got a clear view of my ass through the mirror. Was I being a tease? Absolutely! And I was having a blast.

I nonchalantly looked into the mirror acting as though I didn't notice him looking (which he was very intently). I hooked my fingers into the sides of my thong and slowly began pulling it down, exposing my thick pubic bush. After pulling my thong off I ran my hand through my dark pubic garden and smiled. I then stepped into the shower.

After my shower, I dried myself and dabbed

on just a touch of what I knew was Ben's favorite perfume, then slipped on my gown. Not wanting to make it too obvious that I was trying to seduce him, though my pussy was beginning to get heated and moist (not from the shower water). I ran a brush through my hair and clicked off the bathroom light as I entered the bedroom.

I smiled as it didn't take long to realize my little mirror show delivered the desired effect. Ben was lying in bed, the covers pulled away from his body as he slowly stroked his swollen cock. He smiled when he saw me and ceased his stroking, but maintained his hold on his dick. How I wished I could have taken a picture, he looked so sexy and hot. My cunt grew wet and my clitoris tingled as I gazed at my handsome and obviously horny husband.

"Don't stop on my account, baby," I said, removing my gown and walking nude slowly over to the bed, "Go ahead, baby, stroke it for me! You know how watching you do it turns me on!" I leaned over and kissed him teasingly on the lips. I straddled him and sat back on his thighs.

"Pump it, baby! Beat your meat for me! Do it, baby!" I said as I began to touch myself.

Ben smiled, his eyes full of lust as he resumed his stroking, taking in the sight of me jilling myself off.

"Gina, baby, you look so hot! I wanna fuck you so bad! Watching you in the mirror as you undressed got my dick so hard!" he groaned as he pumped his cock a little faster.

"Were you watching me? You n-naughty boy! Oh-oh, baby! Jerk that dick! You look so sexy, baby!" I panted as I frigged my clit, my breathing becoming deep and shallow.

Ben was jacking off furiously, his eyes glued on me as I masturbated with him.

"Gina! Yeah, baby, I'm gonna cum! Ohhh shit, baby, here it comes-s-s! Ar-rrrgh!" Ben groaned as thick milky ropes of his cum shot from his dick in four impressive spurts landing on his stomach and chest. The last bit dribbled down over his hand and onto his pubes. Watching him cum was the trigger I needed as I too began to cum.

"I'm cumming! I-I-I'm c-cu-cumming! Ohh-Ahh! Fuck!" I panted as my body convulsed with my orgasm. I then collapsed on top of him, his warm cum smearing onto my body. I loved it! We lay there and looked lovingly into each others eyes.

"I love you, Ben! " I said softly.

"I love you too, my Gina!" Ben replied, then we kissed passionately.

After getting a damp rag and cleaning ourselves, we lay in each others arms and slept peacefully.

JANUARY 6th

Ben was sleeping peacefully as I turned off the alarm clock and slipped out of bed. I walked nude to the bathroom and slipped on my robe before walking to the kitchen to prepare a little breakfast for Randy. To my surprise Randy was already up and practically dressed when I went to wake him.

"Hey, breakfast is about ready! How are you this morning?" I said to Randy.

"Okay. I'm good." he mumbled as he slipped his socks on.

After eating a quick breakfast, Randy headed out to catch the bus. I cleaned the breakfast dishes then made a fresh pot of coffee. I drank a couple cups and then headed for a shower. Ben was still sleeping when I eased the door of the bedroom open. I walked quietly to the bathroom and gently shut the door. After a brief shower, I walked back into the bedroom and put on a black thong, some jeans and a navy T-shirt. I walked from the bedroom, gently shutting the door, and headed for the living room. I grabbed my book and sat on the sofa to read.

It was almost 10 am when my cell phone rang. It was Shelly.

"Hey, girl! What's up?" I said as I answered

the phone.

"Hey, GG! Not much, just wanted to call and tell you that I got your photos about done. Girl, I got some really good shots! I'm sure you will be pleased! I know Benny boy will be," She laughed. "I will have them finished this evening, and you can pick them up anytime after 8 in the morning!" Shelly replied.

"That's great! Thank you so much, Shelly! I will be there. Anxious to see them. I still got to run pick up the album to put them in!" I replied.

"Bring it by and I will help you organize it! We can do brunch or something!" she said.

"Sounds great! See ya tomorrow then," I told her and hung up the phone. My heart was beating out of my chest with excitement and my cunt heated. It was nearly 11 when Ben walked into the room fully dressed.

"Gotta go in. Had a couple issues come up,

baby. Not sure what time I will get home tonight, so don't wait up," Ben said as he slipped on his boots.

"Okay. Want something to eat?" I asked, setting my book down.

"No, that's alright! I will pick something up on the way. Love you," he said and walked over and kissed me.

"I love you too, baby! Be careful! Call me later if you get a chance," I said.

"I will!" Ben answered as he walked out the door.

I piddled around the house for a bit then slipped on a pair of flip-flops and drove to Wal-Mart. I purchased a brown photo album, one that has the "window" pocket on the front. It just seemed right to me. On the way home I stopped by my friend Lisa's apartment. She wasn't home, so I headed on home. It was a pretty quiet afternoon for the most part, did some reading and washed some clothes. Alicia called around 3 and we chatted for about 15 minutes. Randy got home a little before 4. Shortly after that Gail called and asked if I would be interested in filling in on Tuesday. I turned her down as I had other "plans".

I fixed supper as Randy completed his homework. We sat down to eat a little after 6. We had meatloaf, cornbread, creamed corn and baked beans. It was really good if I do so myself! We sat in the living room and watched some television, till I sent Randy to bed around 9. I stayed up till around 10:30 and finished the book I had been reading. I hadn't been in bed long, when I heard the front door open. A couple minutes later Ben walked into the bedroom, looking filthy and tired.

"Hey, baby. Poor, baby, you look exhausted!" I said.

"I am. Gotta go back at 5 am tomorrow," he replied.

"Aw! Well go take a shower and come on to bed," I said.

After his shower, he came to bed and I snuggled up next to him.

"I love you sweetheart," I whispered and then kissed his sweet lips.

"I love you too," he murmured back.

We kissed again, and then fell asleep in each others arms.

JANUARY 7th - THE REVEAL!

I awakened just in time to see Ben standing at his dresser, putting his watch on.

"Good morning!" I said, stretching sleepily.

"Good morning! Did I wake you?" he asked then walked over and kissed me.

"No. But I do have to pee!" I replied, then got out of bed and headed for the bathroom.

"Well, I gotta go. Love you," he said. I never get enough of him telling me he loves me!

"Bye, baby. Love you too," I said.

I slipped on my robe, then walked to the

kitchen and poured myself a tall glass of milk. Clicking on the TV, I watched a little of the early morning news. It was around 6:30 when I awakened Randy. He wasn't so easy to wake up this time. I fixed him a little breakfast then off he went. It was after 8 when Cynthia called. She offered to take Randy with her and her son Billy to the movies that evening.

"That would be awesome! Thank you! I owe you one, girl!" I told her. I hadn't been off the phone with Cynthia long when my phone rang again. It was Shelly.

"Hey GG! Well, they are ready! Anytime you wanna come check them out, you can!" she said.

"Great! I can be there in just a few! Unless you're busy?"

"Well, come on, girl! Bring your album with you, I'm anxious for you to see them," Shelly urged.

I slipped on some jeans and a shirt, some flip-flops and out the door I went. I arrived at her studio safely, but in record time. She met me at the door. We walked to the back of her studio, my nerves on edge. She took out the white packet that had my photos and pulled them out.

"Oh my!" I gasped, as I began to look at them.

She was right, they turned out so awesome! I am gonna be honest, I got a little misty-eyed as I looked through them. I just couldn't believe that it was me. I hugged her neck and thanked her once again. She helped me go through and pick out the best ones for the album. The first one she took, while I was still dressed went in the cover window. Before long the album was completed. I visited with Shelly for about an hour and a half before heading for home.

Once I made it home, I went through the album once more. I added sexy little comments underneath each photo (per my dear friend, Ladygarden's, suggestion). I must have thumbed through that album a half dozen times or more. As weird as it may seem, I actually became wet looking at my own photos, as I pictured Ben looking through it and getting a massive erection.

I couldn't wait for Ben to get home so I could present it to him. I decided to wear something sexy when I gave it to him. I decided on the white teddy, white crotchless panties and white fishnet stockings. I figured I would put my hair up in pig tails to finish off the ensemble (wished I would have thought of the pig tails during the shoot!). I nervously texted Ben and asked him to please call and let me know when he would be on his way. I fibbed and told him it was for supper purposes. Moments later he texted me back, saying he would.

My nerves stayed on edge all day, built up with sexual tension. I considered masturbating but decided to save it for my dear husband. I began cleaning house, trying unsuccessfully to take my mind off of it. Before I knew it my son Randy arrived home. I told him about

Cynthia inviting him to go to a movie with her and Billy. He was excited to hear this bit of news.

"You need to get your homework done first though," I told him.

He immediately began working on it as I fixed us a bite to eat. It was a little after six when Cynthia arrived to pick Randy up.

"Why doesn't he just grab some clothes and spend the night at my house. He can catch the bus with Billy," Cynthia said, then smiled and gave me a wink.

Randy eagerly accepted the invitation. Of course I gave my grateful approval. They left shortly after.

"Have fun and behave," I told him then gave him a hug.

"I will, Mom," he replied as he walked out the door.

Everything was falling into place for when Ben would come home. It was a little after 7 when I received the text from Ben that he was on his way. My heart raced as I went to the bedroom and took my planned wardrobe from the bag in the closet and put it on. I went to the bathroom and fixed my hair in cute pig tails, then dabbed on a trace of perfume.

I was ready and extremely horny. It wasn't long before I heard Ben's truck pull up. This was it! The moment of truth had arrived. I stood in the middle of the living room, holding his little gift behind my back and waited for him to walk through that front door. It seemed like it took an eternity, but he finally walked into the house. He stood in the doorway, his eyes big as saucers as he took in my appearance.

A huge grin formed on his face as he said, "Wow, baby, you look really hot! What is the occasion? So beautiful, baby!"

"Well, are you just gonna stand there like a big ox drooling, or are you gonna come in and shut the front door, my handsome stud?" I teased, as I sexily bit a portion of my bottom lip.

He shut the front door and began to remove his shirt, then his boots. He had started to unbuckle his belt when I stopped him.

"Hold on just a minute there, big boy! I have a gift for you. Why don't you have a seat on the couch," I told him.

He was grinning from ear to ear as he walked over and sat down on the sofa. I noticed his growing bulge forming in his jeans. It was difficult for me not to jump him right then, but I maintained my composure despite a very moist cunt.

I walked over to the sofa and said, "Ben, baby, I just want you to know that I love you so very much. You are the best thing that has ever happened in my life, along with our three children of course. You have made me the happiest woman on this planet and I love you for all you do. I love you mostly for loving me and just being you. I wanted to do something special for you, so I had this made for you. I hope you like it."

My hands shook just a bit and I got a little

misty eyed as I handed him the photo album. I sat next to him on the sofa as he looked at the picture on the cover then opened it. He slowly turned each page, reading each of the comments that accompanied each photo.

He looked at me and smiled, then said, "You did this for me, baby? I love it! Such beautiful pictures of you, my baby! I love you so much, my Gina!"

He then kissed me tenderly, our tongues meeting and dancing together. My pussy was so wet, making a wet spot on the sofa. My clit tingled and throbbed.

"I'm so glad you like it, baby! You are my loving man, my husband, and I am your grateful wife. I love you so much," I said then we kissed again.

As we kissed I stroked his thigh, slowly working my hand up to his crotch, feeling the bulge that had formed down his right pants leg. I slowly stroked him through his jeans.

"I want you, baby! I want you right now! You are so beautiful and so fucking sexy!" Ben spoke softly into my ear as he began to kiss my neck and shoulder, his left hand held my right breast.

"I want you too, baby. I so want you. Make love to me, baby," I groaned. We kissed again.

"Sit back, baby!" I purred then rose from the sofa.

I had him open his legs, then got on my knees between them. I ran my hands up his thighs to his crotch and on to his flat stomach. He smiled as my hands finished unbuckling his belt then slowly unzipped his jeans. I looked into his eyes as I reached in and slowly pulled his dick from his jeans. He was practically fully erect as I wrapped my hand around his shaft and began to slowly pump it.

"I love you, baby. I so love this beautiful cock of yours! Look how big and hard it is, baby! It feels so good in my hand… Mm-mm... some pre-cum! I must taste you. Would you like that, baby? Would you like me to suck your big hard dick, baby?" I teased, then leaned forward and kissed the tip, flicking the pre-cum up with my tongue, causing him to groan deeply.

"Gina, baby! YES! Suck me! Suck my hard dick, baby," my husband groaned as I took him into my mouth.

I concentrated on the head at first, then took him deep into my throat. His hand guided my head as I began to bob my head up and down his shaft and I continued sucking his dick.

"Oh-h, Gina! Baby, YES! Suck it! Suck my fat cock! Baby, that feels so good!" Ben groaned, his hand continuing to guide my head as he thrust his hips, fucking my mouth.

I let out a small whimper. My left hand fondled his nuts as I blew him.

"Baby! That feels so good! Gina, baby, I'm not gonna be able to take much more! Baby, your gonna make me cum! I'm gonna cum! I'm gonna cum! Take it! ARRRGH! GR-RRRUMPH!" Ben bellowed as he erupted inside my mouth, coating my tongue and throat with his warm silky cream.

I hungrily swallowed every drop of his baby gravy. Letting him slip from my mouth, I slowly began to kiss my way up his body till our lips met once again. Breaking the kiss, he stood and removed his jeans, standing nude before me.

He leaned forward and kissed my lips, then said, "I'm a little hungry too you know!"

I smiled, my body was more than ready, I so longed for him to taste me! I needed him so badly at that moment, I knew I was probably not gonna last long. I lay on that couch, my legs opened wide for him as he kissed his way down to my swollen wet pussy.

"Oh-h, BEN! Baby, YES!" I groaned as I felt his lips gently kiss my wet pussy lips as he began eating me. I held his head in place as my hips hunched at his sweet mouth and tongue.

"Oh, oh, oh, oh!" I groaned as his talented tongue flicked at my swollen clitoris. My back arched a bit and my hips thrust hard at his mouth. "Cu-Cumming! Baby! BABY! I'M CUUUMMMMMIIINNNG! OHHHH - AHHHH! " I squealed as my body exploded with my orgasm. I panted heavily as my orgasmic wave took my breath. My body convulsed uncontrollably.

It took several moments for me to regain my composure. Ben lay partially on top of me as we kissed and held each other for several minutes.

"Baby, do you want to take this to the bedroom?"

"Sure," I replied, still trying to calm from my orgasm.

Ben got up from on top of me and helped me up from the sofa. My legs felt a bit weak and trembled a bit as I made my way to our bedroom.

"Would you like something to drink, baby?" Ben asked, opening the refrigerator door.

"A glass of wine would be nice," I replied then disappeared into our bedroom.

I removed the teddy, stockings and panties, then got into bed nude. Moments later Ben walked in carrying my drink and his drink as well as the photo album under his arm.

"So, who took the pictures? And what made you decide to make this wonderful gift you have given me, my sweet Gina?" Ben asked as he handed me my drink, then got into bed.

"Shelly took the pictures! She did an awesome job, don't you think, baby!" I replied.

"Wonderful job! Of course she had a beautiful and sexy woman to work with. This is so beautiful and intimate. Thank you again, my baby," Ben said with a smile.

As he thumbed through the album once more I took a sip of wine and said, "You owe Ladygarden a great deal of thanks too, baby. She was the one who inspired me to do it. She did one for her hubby once!" I told him then sat my glass of wine on the bedside table.

I snuggled up next to him and kissed his

shoulder. We lay and looked at the album together.

"Touch me. Baby, play with my dick! Make me hard, baby," Ben said as he continued to thumb through the album.

I reached down and took his limp dick into my hand and began to massage it, occasionally tickling his nuts. Slowly but surely it began to thicken. He continued to look at the pictures as I continued to pump on his cock with my hand. Before long he was rock hard, his hips hunched slightly as I slowly beat his meat.

Ben set the album on his side table and said, "Let's fuck! Get up here and ride my cock, baby. Give me some of that sweet pussy!"

We kissed as I mounted him, positioning myself over his large erection. Holding it up with my left hand I slowly eased down upon it.

"Oh, Ben!" I moaned softly as I took his eight inches into me, until he was in to the hilt, filling me.

I began to ride him, working my hips in a circular motion grinding my clit so deliciously onto his pubic bone. It felt oh-so-good. His hands fondled both my breasts, tweaking both my nipples making them firm and erect. The bed creaking and groaning, as well as our breathing and occasional moans and groans were the only sounds as we continued to screw.

"That's it, baby, ride my cock! Such a hot cunt! Ride me, baby, fuck it feels so good! Get you some dick, baby! You like that dick, don't you, baby?" He moaned, "My baby loves to fuck, don't you, baby?" Ben said, his words fueling my passion.

I began to hump him, riding up and down his hard cock. I propped myself with my arms on either side of him as I looked upon his face as we fucked.

"YES! Oh YES, I love it! Oh-h, Ben, your dick feels so good! Fuck! Fuck! Fuck! Mmmmph, Oh, oh-ah! B-baby, I'm gonna cum! Gonna cum all over your big fucking dick! OHHHHHH-AHHHHHH!" I cried as I came, collapsing on top of my love, my body trembled.

Ben rolled me onto my back and mounted me. I opened my legs wide as he guided his hard penis to the mouth of my still pulsating cunt.

"Mmmmph, BABY!" I squealed as he pushed his hard dick back inside me balls deep.

He began to thrust hard and deep causing small grunts to escape my lips as he pounded into me. "I'm gonna fuck this cunt good, baby! So fucking good! Gina, baby! Such a hot pussy!" Ben groaned as he continued to fuck me hard, his nuts slapping hard against my ass.

"MMM-MMPH! F-F-FUCK, MMMMPH, M-M-MEEEEEEE! OHHHHHH-AHHHHH! BAAAAAABY!" I screamed as I began to cum once again.

"OHHHHHH FUUUCK!" Ben roared as he spasmed and shot his nut deep inside me.

We lay there with him on top of me, his cock

still buried deep inside me. Both of us covered in our passion sweat, gasping for air. After a few minutes he slipped out and roll off of me.

After regaining our senses, we had worked up an appetite. We got out of bed and walked nude to the kitchen. We fixed a sandwich for each of us. We sat at the table and ate. After eating we both enjoyed a couple glasses of wine apiece. We lay in bed and enjoyed a few minutes of nude cuddling.

"Hey, baby, how about sucking my dick for a bit!" Ben said softly.

"Sure." I replied as we then kissed.

I began to slowly kiss my way down his body, kissing and tracing every inch of his chest and abdomen with my tongue until I reached his wonderful cock and meaty balls. I took his limp dick into my hand and began massaging it, then lightly kissed the tip. I flicked my tongue over the head then down the underside of his shaft all the way to his balls. I began to tongue his nuts, gently taking each one into my mouth tonging each one thoroughly as I pumped his cock with my right hand. I even tongued that spot between his ball sack and asshole (this drives him nuts!). Moving back to his dick, which was slowly beginning to swell. I took it into my mouth and proceeded to suck him.

"YES, that's it! Ohh, baby, you're such a wonderful cocksucker!" Ben said as he guided my head with his hand. He soon had raised another hard on thanks to my oral stimulation. "OK, baby! Get on your hands and knees for me! I wanna play with that hot ass of yours."

I did as he requested and got on my hands and knees. Actually resting on my forearms with my ass up in the air for his enjoyment. He got up on his knees behind me and began to grope and knead my ass cheeks.

"You love that ass! Don't you, baby?" I said as I looked back at him.

"You know I do, baby! You got a fine looking ass," Ben replied, as he gave his cock a couple pumps with one hand.

"Kiss it! Kiss my ass, baby! Show me how much you love my ass!" I said as I ran a hand to my cunt and slowly rubbed my clitoris.

I moaned softly as I felt his warm lips upon my ass. He then spread my ass cheeks and ran his finger over my asshole, tickling it.

"YES! Finger it! Finger my butt! I love it, baby!" I said as I fingered my wet cunt. "Baby! Ohhhh, baby, yes! Ohh, you dear man! Yessss! Ohhhh fuuuucckk!" I squealed as I felt his moist tongue flick at my asshole, I came fast as he tongued my tight hole. "Baby, please! Fuck me! Fuck me now! Put your hard dick into me! Please fuck me hard!" I panted.

"You want my dick in your hot cunt, baby! I'll give it to you!" Ben said then pushed his cock deep into my pussy in one hard thrust.

"Mmm-mphh! Yes! Give it to me! Ohh, Ben, baby. Fuck my cunt! Oh, YES!" I cried as Ben held my hips with both hands and pumped me hard and deep. "Ohhh-aahhh!" I groaned as I exploded with another body wrenching orgasm.

Ben continued to fuck me hard for a few more minutes before he himself came. Groaning deeply, we collapsed beside each other totally spent and exhausted. It was nearly 3 am. Ben had to be at work at 5am. But he never complained.

I so love my Ben! Some may not agree with what I did or how I did it. But it definitely paid off in the long run for both of us.

ABOUT THE AUTHOR

GG or HornyGG—as known on the Marriage Heat website—is a happily married mother of there. God bless you, my reader, and stay horny for your spouse!

5816155R00072

Printed in Great Britain
by Amazon.co.uk, Ltd.,
Marston Gate.